Frequency 16
by h.e. newell

Copyright © 2021 h.e. newell.

All rights reserved. No part of this publication may be reproduced, distributed, or transmitted, in any form or by any means, including photocopying, recording, or other electronic or mechanical methods, without the prior written permission of the author, except in the case of brief quotations embodied in critical reviews and certain other noncommercial uses permitted by copyright law. For permission requests, write to throneroomjewel@gmail.com

Any references to historical events, real people, or places are used fictitiously. Names, characters, and places are products of the author's imagination.

Book Layout © 2016 BookDesignTemplates.com

With special thanks to Chalom for creating the original cover art. Please visit or follow on Instagram to experience more of this deeply anointed, gifted artist.

Dedication

For everyone who has ever been trapped in a moment and set free in another. You are not alone. Embrace your gifts and tell your story.

For my kindred hearts, who dwell in the frequencies of Heaven. Whose vibrations keep me grounded…

And always, for the One who created everything in a Word.

h.e. newell

Frequency 16

It happened late one night...

    At sixteen-second intervals, the warm water faucet in the enamel kitchen sink drips as it has done for the last three years. It's most likely a worn-out washer or gasket. Normal people call a plumber to fix it, but Albert puts a glass under it to measure how much water is wasted in a day. Don't ask him why. He will say things like, "The cadence of the drip is accompanied by the perfect intonation of the wasted water drops filling the glass. It gives one the impression that every sixteen seconds something was added to, or removed from, the atmosphere."

    It just sounds like "bloop, bloop, bloop" to me, but I'll take it. Thick and sterile silence always fills his house, otherwise. Some days the sound becomes increasingly annoying depending on who you ask.

For example, if you ask Albert, he'll tell you that the measure kept by the wasted water drops is an ambient metronome by which he sets his life. It keeps him mindful of the value of sixteen seconds.

On the other hand, if you ask me, I'll have no problem saying, "No one cares about a dripping faucet. No one cares how much water is wasted in a day. All they need to know is that the noise is friggan annoying!".

We're as different as oil and water, but I tend to think that's what makes us so perfect for one another.

Albert decided long ago that our relationship was best treasured privately. Wimp. He has no sense of adventure. Like right now; he's making no short task of scolding me as he clears the dinner dishes.

"Did you have to call that man a dumbass?" He scrapes the plate of spinach, chicken, and strawberry salad I've barely touched into the sink. "You'll have me beaten up in the street someday."

"You don't think he deserved it just a little?"

Albert had come out of the Food Mart with a paper sack full of groceries when he realized he couldn't access his driver's side door. A monster of a truck had come along after him and parked ridiculously close. He was just deciding to climb across from my side when the vehicle's owner showed up. So, of course, I felt I had to share my thoughts on the situation.

"Maybe you should keep a case of friggan can openers in your back seat, so you can leave one for the next guy you decide to park next to!" I railed at Monster truck guy.

"Amanda, shut your mouth!" Albert hissed.

"What did you just say?" Monster-truck guy was shocked, to say the least.

"You heard me, dumbass! There are three empty spots right there, but you parked next to us like a moron. Stop overcompensating for your tiny pecker; go buy a Chevette and learn how to drive!" I shouted as I flipped off the bonehead who had at least fifty pounds over Albert. "Use *that* to clean the wax out of your ears while you're at it!"

"Do I need to kick your ass?" he asked, stepping closer to Albert.

"No. No butt-kicking necessary. I can wait until you move your, uh, truck." Albert cleared his throat and stepped back.

"Damn right you will."

Monster-truck guy climbed into his oversized truck and peeled out of the spot, nearly hitting me.

"Idiot! Come back and try that again!" I shouted as Albert got in the car. The truck came to a screeching halt and began to back up. "Come on, Al! Let's go!" I shouted. I couldn't stop laughing as he sped off to avoid another confrontation.

"People deserve a lot of things." He plunges a teacup into the dish basin, scrubs it, and rinses it under the water running on the other side. "That doesn't mean it's your responsibility to give it to them."

"Yes, it is." I snap my gum and wink at him.

Frequency 16

Rinsing the rest of the dishes, he listens to me talk about how long I've lived in the city and how much worse the idiots like Monster-truck guy are becoming. Eventually, I trail off into a quiet that Albert greatly appreciates. He cleans the sink, sets the glass back under the dripping faucet, and comes into the living room. I'm falling asleep. Albert forgives me by the time he finishes pulling a blanket over me and disappears to his bedroom.

I know he hopes I'll wake up and take myself home.

At eleven thirty-two and sixteen seconds, the "bloop, bloop, bloop" lulls him to sleep.

At two sixteen in the morning, he wakes up to the sound of pots and pans clanging. He grumbles, pulling a shirt over his head as he shuffles to the kitchen.

I'm so irritated, I slam the refrigerator door.

"No friggan butter. Who the heck eats this low-fat crap?"

"Apparently someone does, or they wouldn't sell it," he counters, relieving me of the low-fat crap. "Don't you have a home?"

"Yours was closer," I answer automatically because I anticipated the question. "And I can't drive anymore."

"It was so nice and quiet; I thought you'd left."

"Thought or hoped?"

"Probably both," he supplies, after contemplating which answer would pacify me. On nights like this, it's difficult to know. But then, he has moments when he has no problem chastising me. "You're causing horribly negative frequencies that aren't good for the baby. I wish you'd stop."

"You're just pissed because I'm louder than your annoying, dripping tap." I point to the sink with disdain. "I just don't get it, Al." Hopping up onto the counter, I cross my legs and watch him.

"It's calming." He lifts the glass and sets it on the counter, being careful as though he were moving a Faberge egg. "What is it you want to eat?"

"An omelet." I pout. "You have no butter for the pan, just *that*."

Frequency 16

"Aunt Jane left it here when she came last week. Blame her." He takes a carafe of oil from the cupboard and pulls a chef's knife from the magnetic strip on the wall. Rhythmically, he begins to dice yellow peppers and onions. Everything with Albert is a dance and he really has no idea. "Mushrooms?"

"No, they make me puke."

"Tomatoes?"

"Yeah, and some capers. I know you have that fancy stuff."

"Capers it is." Without speaking, he pours avocado oil into the pan and whips the eggs as he cracks them one by one into a bowl. "What kind of cheese do you want?"

"Surprise me. Just not cheap, processed crap."

"Right."

I know he has the sound of the wasted water drops ingrained in his mind, and he's creating a symphonic masterpiece in his head while he's sauteeing the vegetables. It's what he does with everything. He crumbles a piece of imported, Bulgarian feta and adds the pattern it makes to his mental composition. He's making sure to remind himself to try and translate this into music later. As he goes through the motion of making the omelet, he half listens to me talk about how glad I am that I quit my job at the advertising firm and what sort of bulbs I should plant around the lamp post.

"The baby should like this," he says as he hands me the plate.

"I hope so. "Kaptin Berger" is getting old."

"You've been pregnant for over three years now, when are you due?"

The pan hisses as he wipes it down with a wet cloth.

"I'm twenty-eight weeks and don't be a douche." Like a vulture, I address the plate while Albert cleans up after himself.

Setting the glass back in the sink, he surveys the tidy kitchen with great satisfaction. Everything is just the way he likes it; in its place and settled. He needs things this way so he can think. I learned a long time ago that the vibrations and frequencies of anything being out of place are too much for him. He can't sleep at night or work during the day. This is why he began his own company from his home studio, and why he seldom has anyone to his house. When we were kids, it made him feel like he was in a tornado, and the chaos gave him headaches. On the other hand, when everything is calm and in its place, when everyone is doing what they need to do in their own space, he feels secure. Nestled in the eye of things.

Keep in mind that Albert isn't about the business of controlling the things around him, or mastering his environment. He's about the business of creating serenity. There isn't anything serene about cooking caper and feta omelets in the middle of the night. It just kept me from creating tension. There's no controlling me, and Albert knows it. He always tells me I operate on an impossible frequency to harness. And while Albert's ultimate goal is to stay in the solitude of his own world, he also says that my more complex frequency provides him with just enough contrast to keep things interesting.

To be honest, I'm not completely sure what that all means. Hearing myself repeat it all just makes me feel like I have a fraction of Albert's intelligence.

"Have you gone out with that girl from Steve's office yet?" I pick up the last crumbs of the omelet with a fingertip. "He said she was interested in you."

"No. And I probably won't." He takes my plate and sets it in the dishwasher. He'll take it out and wash it by hand in the morning. "She's too *pretty*."

"*What* are you even talking about? Have you *looked* at yourself lately?" I hop off the counter and play with his collar. "You just flip this hair a little and a new shirt…"

"Quit that." He blushes and swats my hands away.

"Why? Are you afraid someone might actually go out with you?"

"No." He sees my raised eyebrow and confesses. "Fine. Yes. Are you happy?"

"Of course I'm not happy. You should meet someone nice, go out on one friggan date in your life, and maybe have a nice time."

"Why do that when I have you?" Albert's sarcasm makes me smile. "People don't understand me."

"So, you either think I understand you or you don't think I'm *people*." Even knowing what he means, I can't pass an opportunity to get him going. "Gees, Al, one girl cheats on you and I'm given the life sentence of being your only female companion 'til the day you die?"

"When you put it like that… Well, you sound unfeeling when you put it like that."

"All the OCD and brainwaves crap aside," I say.

"Frequencies."

"Sorry, *frequencies*. All the OCD and *frequencies* crap aside, you could have a normal life with friends and girls and parties. Everywhere he goes they're asking about you, Steve says." My attempt to encourage him backfires, I put his collar back the way it was and smooth back his hair. "What's happened to you, Al?"

"Nothing." His nostrils flare and the vein in his forehead begins to pulse. "Nothing! I just like everything the way it was!"

Albert seldom becomes upset or loses his temper. When he does it's quiet and almost undetectable, with the occasional outburst. Like the time that his mom washed his laundry (rather than send it out for him) and shrunk all his wool sweaters. Somehow, she thought he wouldn't notice. Of course, he got them during his semester in Scotland and he noticed immediately. He blew up at her and shocked everyone. The more incensed he became with her lack of understanding his upset at breaking the rhythm of his routine, the more I cheered him on like he was running for a touchdown.

There was also the unfortunate occasion when his former girlfriend, Kelsey, stood him up for an important dinner his company was giving. She told him that her roommate was sick with chickenpox and that she felt she might be coming down with them herself. Being a totally old-fashioned gentleman, Albert decided that since he already had chickenpox at age nine, he'd take them some carry-out dinner. Imagine his surprise when Albert showed up and learned that not only was Kelsey's roommate in Florida for a month but that Kelsey was entertaining the lawyer who had recently hired her to be his paralegal.

After Albert put his fist through her bedroom door, he went home and burnt everything she left at his house. He sent it to her via courier when the ashes cooled. The

Frequency 16

package should have sent a clear message but she still calls him from time to time.

Truth be told, Albert hates the lower, negative vibration that losing his temper, shouting, punching, or arguing creates. He's done extensive study on the effects of these "bad frequencies" and foul language on house plants, jars of water, fabric, people, and animals. From everything he's read or discovered on his own, he concluded that anger, sarcasm, and aggression (all the things that make life interesting) actually breaks down fiber, makes water bitter to the taste, kills plants, and possibly alters DNA. He's used everything from blood to firewood to a pure gold ingot to conduct his research.

Most recently, he's been working closely with an old college friend of his to determine the effects of certain musical frequencies on cancerous cells. He's scheduled to present his findings to the board at the University in sixteen days.

None of that means he doesn't feel anything negative. He says he just doesn't want to release bad vibrations. I tend to move through life without filters. You'd think this is a problem for Albert, but it's quite the opposite.

He tells people his favorite thing about our relationship is the way that, as he puts it, "Amanda embodies the balance between negative and positive vibrations." When we were kids he told my dad that my negative frequencies made it possible for him to "create balanced and calming rhythms and vibrations". To put this into perspective for you, we were eight years old.

     Once he admitted he was jealous of my ability to operate in both frequencies without even realizing I was doing it.

     As I step back and study him, I can see subtle ways his mood is changing. I don't pretend to understand all this vibration science, or why he's so obsessed with it, but I do know that it's his way of responding to everything happening around him. I also know this isn't the best time to tease him about it.

     "Al. Why so touchy?"

     "Well, you won't leave me alone about it! You're irritating me." He fixes his hair the way he likes it and digs through a drawer for a piece of chocolate. As he calms down, he confesses,

Frequency 16

"I met someone I like. We talk every day, actually."

"And? Does she have a name?" I close the blinds and turn on lights on the desk and over the kitchen table.

"Lia. She's twenty-six, works in music production, graduated from Loyola. Anything else, *detective*?" He bites into the chocolate and throws the wrapper into the garbage.

"When are you going to see her?" I'm intrigued now, so I sit on the kitchen table and open a bag of potato chips. "Bro! I want all the juicy details," I demand with a mouth full of barbeque flavored chips.

He cringes to see me shove my hand in the bag and put another handful of chips into my mouth.

"We had lunch the other day."

"No, you didn't."

"Okay, I'm lying."

"What the heck? You're just telling me now?" I throw a potato chip at him as though it might wound him. "How long have I been here?"

"You're difficult to talk to these days, with mini you coming and all." He spreads a paper towel on the table and takes a handful of chips. They have to be the same size or he puts them back. "I've been out with her quite a bit. We went to a few movies, and that Thai place you hate."

"And?"

"She had a hot pot and I had fish heads. It was all very romantic. What do you want me to say, Amanda?" He takes more potato chips, avoiding my gaze. "Okay, I had that insanely spicy curry with the squid in it that you say makes the car stink after."

"It does, but you know that's not what I mean."

Crumbs fly across the table as I speak. I have to admit, I do these uncouth things on purpose. I like to wind him up.

"And she has wonderful table manners." He dodges another lethal potato chip and stands up. "She's pretty and smart, and she is coming over tomorrow. Today rather. She's got an idea for the piece I'm working on."

Albert letting someone into the inner workings of his creative mind is unheard of.

"Wow. That's big for you!"

"I know." He paces at the head of the table and runs his fingers through his hair. "What am I going to do? The whole vibration here is going to change to something brand new."

I hit the table.

"Would you forget the feng shui crap for a minute and tell me what you're going to do on your date?"

"We're going to sit at the piano and finish a song?" he offers. "She's producing that short film I'm doing music for. I got stuck," Albert shrugs.

Now he's admitting that he asked her to help him compose? Pigs across America have sprouted wings.

"You have to do something special."

"Get out the espresso maker?"

"Stop being coy." I dig through the bowl of nuts in the middle of the table, spilling an assortment of peanuts, cashews, and hazelnuts all over the place. I don't stop until I find a Brazil nut. "Do you even remember what she looks like?"

"As a matter of fact, I do." He eats another piece of chocolate, refusing to look at the mess I've made. "She's a little shorter than you, and not so curvy. Her eyes are phenomenal; almond-shaped and deep brown, and they smile when she does. And she's got black curly hair. You know, those tight curls like Rae Dawn Chong. Pretty teeth, perfect skin the color of a latte. She told me her dad is Bahamian and her mom is Korean." He waits to see if he passed my test.

It's the strangest thing about Al; he could tell you what I looked like, or wore, at all times. Yet, he was robbed in broad daylight on a trip to Manhattan, and couldn't tell the police how tall the mugger might have been. The day after finding Kelsey and her boss in bed, he had already forgotten that she had strawberry blonde hair and was missing part of her left index finger. Albert even forgot what the vice president of his old company looked like, and inadvertently told him what a twit he thought he was. But there has never been an occasion where he couldn't describe me.

If you ask him, Albert usually says I'm pretty in a strong and Germanic sort of way with high cheekbones and a straight, angled nose. I wear a tiny diamond in my left nostril. My eyes aren't quite round and not quite almond-shaped, and some days are greener than others. My hair is thick and falls halfway down my back. He even tells people I lighten it so that when summer comes I look like I spend all my time at the shore.

"She's five foot eight and not thinly framed, with perfectly placed, subtle curves," he told the doorman at the club we lost each other in. Depending on the mood he's in or who's asking he can tell you what all of my tattoos are and where I had them done.

I'm not that eloquent. When I describe him, I normally use words like buff, dorky, and "Clark Kentish", all in the same breath. He has a few tattoos that I managed to talk him into over the years, but he's never had the nerve to pierce anything. When pressed, I once told someone that he was six foot one, with wavy brown hair and brown eyes, and nothing more of interest. The truth? Albert is stunning.

There's nothing uninteresting about him; I'm just overly protective.

Right now, behind this façade, I'm trying not to be overly protective of him again. I'm impressed. It makes me smile to know he's met someone he likes this much, so I roll with it.

"You *do* like her." I get up to stretch my back and look for a napkin. "You can't blow this, Al. Seriously."

"Why do you say that?"

"You sabotage *everything* ever since…" I stop myself.

It's too late. Albert's completely rigid, frozen with his back to me, one hand on the counter, the other in the tall cupboard reaching for something. I know this body language, and I know it doesn't happen often. I only have a second to register it before he spins around so fast it startles me.

"What the hell do you know? *You're* the one who sabotaged everything." He throws the napkins at me and the package splits when it hits me, leaving ninety-seven soft white, disposable dinner napkins fluttering to the floor like oversized snowflakes. "You ruined the vibration of everything!"

Even though he's escalating, I know I need to stay calm and act unphased.

"Oh, please. I single-handedly threw the universe out of balance? I'm awesome, but I have limits."

I pick up a napkin and leave the rest scattered across the floor.

"*You're* the one who had to go off with Mr. Football and leave me behind!" He shouts this time.

"You hate football! You came to one game, and all you did was measure every sixteen seconds and complain about how there were *no discernable patterns* to the game. I had to drink an extra beer just to get through the first quarter." Pausing to think for a second, I add, "I suppose that's not entirely true; I usually drink like that."

"Nervous babbling." He narrows his eyes. "You were on a date, Amanda. I felt so left out."

"You never told me."

"You wouldn't have listened. But then you went and *married* him and where did that leave me?"

As calmly as possible, Albert cleans up the napkins, potato chips, and mixed nuts I've got all over the table.

"You could've tried to get to know Steve," I say finally.

"His vibrations were off just slightly. I couldn't stand it sometimes." He tosses everything in the trash can and looks for another piece of chocolate. This chocolate eating thing is new. "And anyway...what sort of person would I have been if I complained when you finally found someone who flips off bad drivers, jokes about saggy balls, and hurls emotionally damaging insults at the Cleveland Browns?"

I have to admit, Steve is perfect. Unfortunately, Albert has no idea how much Steve has wanted to bond with him. So much so, that he agreed to have Al for our best man. Let me just say it made for one of the most awkward wedding weekends in history, I'm sure.

"You tolerate me, let's be honest," I hear him saying.

"Tolerate you? No." I pick up the glass full of wasted water and hold it in front of him.

Frequency 16

"*This* kind of crap I tolerate because it's part of your weird, quirky, adorable psychopathicness that I love so much. You; I do not tolerate."

"Put that down."

"Take back what you said about me tolerating you."

"Fine, I take it back."

"You can't take it back, even I know that."

"I know. Once I said it, it started its vibration. Maybe there's enough fluid around the baby so it won't feel it." He's visibly upset at having said it in the first place, so I leave it alone. When I refuse to put the glass down, he becomes antsy. "You didn't tolerate me, I'm sorry."

"Forgiven," I concede. "What's so special about this glass, Al?"

Again, he shifts gears. He clears his throat and prepares to get philosophical on me. I don't mind; it's endearing in its own way.

"Take a moment to consider what sort of glass it could be that would faithfully stand in someone's sink collecting the wasted water drops caused by the loose washer in the hot water faucet this entire time," he says.

h.e. newell

    Can anyone else make an old glass and a leaky tap sound so poetic? Let me try.

    This glass has stood faithfully for three years in the sink, collecting the drips that Albert so deeply treasures every sixteen seconds. Standing at sixteen ounces, making the great experiment of waste measurement redundant, the glass is clear with the slightest hint of green to it, a trumpet-like rim at the top and a sort of lily shape overall. It was the last glass left of a set of eight his parents bought on their first wedding anniversary. Thirty-three years ago these glasses were the height of fashion, and his mom proudly placed them on the dinner table every evening until the first one broke. After that, his dad bought a new set and the seven survivors got stuffed to the back of the cupboard.

    At the tender age of seven when Albert first realized that these glasses had musical potential, he forbid his mom to give them to the white elephant sale at the local Methodist church. He filled them at different levels, experimenting with liquids of varying thickness and gooeyness, and rubbed his fingers along the rims in the same way as the Tibetan bowls he would discover eight years later. He dripped and dropped all sorts of things into the glasses as they stood full, half full, half empty. He learned the tone, pitch, and frequency of each sound and memorized all of it. His mom called him obsessive, his dad called him creative, and his aunt Jane called him a genius. True to form, I called him things like bat ears and freak show. But I defied anyone else to make fun of him or suffer a broken face.

    Over the years, one glass after another broke, leaving Albert with this last surviving member of his original ensemble. It took him several months to figure out how to find it the perfect use. He felt like he had to protect that last glass from meeting the same death as the other seven. It became a way to maintain some kind of memory or connection to everything in his life before yesterday.

    "It's the last one," he says. "Every sixteen seconds it catches a drop of that wasted water from the hot side of the faucet and makes the perfect sound."

"I don't understand." I drink from the glass. "So my baby just drank perfect sounding water?"

"Possibly. Your baby is surrounded by water right now. Every oscillation is perfect for him or her while they're playing at Submariner in there." He keeps his eyes on the glass. "That's why sonograms or ultrasounds can make pictures for you to see your spleen or blood vessels or in this case, your baby. They send inaudible frequencies into the water and it bounces back, making a picture. Why do you think they wanted you to drink so much before you had your appointment?" He waits to see if I'll consider his explanation. "Anyway it's not the water that sounds perfect, it's the whole process that makes the sound."

"Why sixteen, Al?"

"What do you mean?"

"Why did you fix the faucet to drip within sixteen seconds?"

"I didn't."

"Man, don't lie to me. You searched for "Why is my faucet dripping?" on your laptop."

Frequency 16

I drink more. "You could have had it fixed, but you timed it instead. Why did you do that?"

"I like the rhythm."

"*Sixteen* seconds?" I finish the water and hold the glass up again. "Not fifteen. Not seventeen. *Sixteen*."

"So?"

"Is that our frequency or something?" I ask. I have a theory, but he's surprised me so many times during this conversation I'm open to anything. "Frequency sixteen?

"God, Amanda! *Not* frequency sixteen! No!" Is that panic in his eyes? Disbelief? I can't tell. For the first time in our lives, without a few drinks in him, Albert is stammering, stumbling over words. His hands are everywhere; in his hair, rubbing his chest, mimicking a graph. He's explaining something about Chaney, Parks, and Snyder in the early 1960s, and he's so put off, I can't decipher through his technical, snooty falooty language. "16 Hz is one of the most annoying frequencies. In 1969 the US Navy even did a study and documented it. Subjects said it was alarming!"

"You've never told me this before." He shrugs as his breathing calms. "So…you think I'm annoying?"

"What? No!"

"What, then?"

"I need to find the perfect frequency. The perfect vibration. *Our* frequency. It's out there somewhere." His hands float across the air as though they're following the lines of a sound wave. He's followed that sort of technology since he got his first computer and the music player showed the sound waves while songs played. "Our rhythm, melody, everything…I just need to find it." He makes a motion as if he's catching something in the air.

"Like Wholetones?" I ask.

He smiles in the way he has when I'm understanding this world he's created for himself.

"Something like that. 528Hz is divisible by 16."

"Why sixteen?"

"That's our number." Albert takes another glass out of the cupboard and sets it in the enamel sink under the dripping hot water faucet. "Yours and mine."

"You have to stop doing this, Al." I walk away from the sink, still carrying the glass. "It's been three years; you have to knock this crap off."

"How do I do that?" He tries a different glass in the sink. "How do I forget our number? Just like that?" Albert snaps his fingers. "A person doesn't cease to exist like that, Amanda."

"No, I guess they don't." I put the glass on the desk and start to look through the envelope full of pictures. I find the one I want. "Have you got a pen? You know when we were kids, I was always jealous of you."

"Me? You were the popular one, always having a good time."

He hands me a pen and clears a space at the desk.

"You were always in your head, figuring things out, seeing things like a cyborg or something." I stop and look at him for a long time. "You remember that movie where the machine came back through time and they showed the little screen that processed everything he saw?"

"*The Terminator?*"

"Yeah. I always pictured your mind like that." I look at the glass and consider how important it is to him. "Everything was pretty finite in my world, but yours was limitless. I used to wait for the words to come out of your mouth like in *Yellow Submarine*."

"There was *nothing* predictable about you." Albert sits on the floor and starts counting sit-ups. "Not that you were a scatterbrain or anything like that. You just lived a pretty deliberate life."

"I liked jumping in feet first."

"Thirteen. Fourteen. To say the least. Sixteen."

"We were friends."

"You always looked out for me." He counts four more sit-ups. "It's not my fault that changed."

"You were such a beautiful boy. So oblivious and shy; all the girls tried to get me to see if you'd take them out." I laugh to think of it. "I always liked that."

"I guess they did do that."

Over the years, I always took the natural position of protector, go-between, and counselor when it came to Al. Particularly with the opposite sex. Maybe because I was older, or maybe because I knew he was vulnerable in ways most guys aren't. Who can say? When we were kids, it was normal to find Albert off to the side making a world around himself. I'd convince everyone that Albert's ideas were the most fun. In the end, we had a better time and got into less trouble when we played whatever game he'd come up with.

In middle school, I got into hellacious mischief. Albert often took responsibility for whatever it was, claiming he put me up to it for a scientific hypothesis or other curiosity. Because everyone knew he was a little different that way, I rarely got punished.

In high school, Albert had no understanding of how good looking he was. He had so little grasp of it, that he never noticed the gaggles of girls who sat on the porch with me while he cut the grass. He did this every Saturday and Tuesday afternoon at two o'clock in the heat of the summer, oblivious to their presence. He told me that the pattern of the grass, the sweat running down his skin, the vibration of the mower, and the stimulation of his muscle tissue worked together to create a frequency that he found "absolutely fascinating".

For a hundred and twelve days, he cut the acre and a half of grass around the house; even the downward slope near the creek. He'd play a cd in his headphones and decide how it worked with the vibration of the mower. Sometimes Beethoven and sometimes Daft Punk; he quickly discovered that the perfect music depended on his mood that day. He said he "learned to be obedient to that to gain the optimal benefit of the whole experience". Years later when I told him about my friends, he was amazed. All those years he just assumed that we had nothing else to do, so we sat on the veranda and waited for him.

"You're talking like I've died." Albert counts five more sit-ups. "I'm still shy, I hate trying to talk to people."

"You're still beautiful and perfect." I turn away from him and write on the back of the picture. "I think you're a perfect vibration in and of yourself."

"Damn, I lost count."

"Forty-eight."

"Thank you. Do you suppose Lia might think so, too?" He takes up where he left off.

"She'd be a fool not to."

"Steve's always talking about how smart and beautiful you are. He's good for you." Albert stops at sixty-four. "I guess you need that."

This admission is a huge step for him, but I don't acknowledge that.

"Here you go with the sixteens again." I finish writing on the picture and stand up. "You have to stop, Al."

"I can't help it." He turns to his stomach and begins to count push-ups. "It's not fair of you to treat me like I do it on purpose."

"You're right, it's not." I take the glass off the desk and circle the room while he counts to sixty-four again. "Don't hate me for this," I say quietly.

"How could I ever hate you?"

Suddenly, I'm Nolan Ryan, and I throw the glass as hard as I can against the cupboard under the sink. In one motion, Albert jumps up to avoid the bits of glass. They're all over the mat and embedded into the cupboard door.

"What are you doing?!" He hops back to avoid the broken glass. "Do you even know what kind of reverberation you just caused? You can't *do* things like that!" He paces, wringing his hands and trying desperately to listen for the frequency I've just disrupted. He stops and looks at me with a strange marriage of panic and confusion washing over him. "It's gone now. What am I going to do?"

"Make a new one." I crouch down to clean up the mess.

"All those sixteen-second increments. Gone."

"You can't save every drop of water, Albert."

"They aren't just drops of water. It's lost time." He looks at the wall clock, and I know he's watching the second hand. "It's those sixteen minutes that you left me alone! That

Frequency 16

broke our vibration. I need them back so I can-."

"You *can't have* those minutes back, Al. You've been trying your whole life." Brushing the cupboard door with a wet paper towel, I wipe off the bits of glass out of the wood and throw them in the trash can. "I wish things were different, but they are what they are. Maybe we never had a frequency."

"No! That's not true. Every sound, every vibration is perpetual, even if it becomes far enough away that we can't hear it anymore." He walks deliberately around me as I clean the floor and roll up the mat. "*We had a frequency.* It goes through me every time my heart pumps."

"Exactly. So, you didn't need that glass anymore." He's wrestling with the panic, the tension of it is tangible. I know him so well, there's only one way for him to work this through to a resolution. I suggest, "Why don't you translate it into music?"

"Into music." He paces sixteen steps, nibbling on the side of his thumb, turns, and paces sixteen steps in the opposite direction. He's either counting time or listening for a melody. He does this three times before he speaks again. "I could do that."

"Yes, and you could play it any time you want." I wash my hands and put the glass from the sink into the drain board. "Other people could hear it and know our story."

"I'll play it for the baby," he says from some place in his corner of the universe even I have no access to.

When he was eight, Albert composed his first cohesive piece of music. It was based on a day at the beach. Every August, a gazillion jellyfish wash up on the Atlantic coast to mate or congregate or whatever social habits jellyfish have. We watched Albert's grandmother stab countless jellyfish through with a stick as she walked along the drainpipe. That night, Al had a dream that a giant jellyfish came along and poked her through with a stick of its own. He woke up and scribbled down some music notes in the middle of the night. The next morning, he borrowed the neighbor's guitar and composed a piece of music that turned out to be sixteen minutes long.

Keep in mind that a jellyfish is composed of ninety-five percent water. Humans, nearly sixty. Jellyfish are essentially brainless, functioning sacks of water. Humans are far more complex.

Al has researched pregnancy thoroughly. At twenty-eight weeks my unborn, two-and-a-quarter-pound baby is happily swimming in "approximately eight hundred milliliters of body temperature fluid which is safely, and quite remarkably, encased in a thin membrane within your womb."

I wonder if Albert is jealous of me for having total access to a personal scientific experiment. In his way, I'm sure he's envying my baby for "having access to such an incredible environment of sounds and vibrations". His words, not mine.

He's always been fascinated by this sort of thing. More than once, Albert has gone swimming after rowing practice. He just floats with his ears submerged to try and better understand how his voice and other noises sound to mini-me. He says he's certain that water distorts frequencies, but he's still very careful to make sure that he only releases positive and healthy vibrations when I'm around.

I'll never admit this to Al, but it wasn't until I lost fifty-seven percent of my hearing that I even remotely understood his obsession with sound vibrations. He has studied all of it; oscillation, echolocation, and things no one's ever heard of. I give him a hard time, but I pay attention to everything he tells me. In fact, on more than one occasion, in secret, I've laid my head on the surface of the counter when the dishwasher ran. There is definitely a rhythm to stuff like that. Sometimes I set my palms flat on the television screen when my favorite program comes on just to feel the sounds. Last week the baby jumped around when the "Buckaroo Bonsai" theme song started playing.

Since I understand that to *really* hear whatever music Al comes up with as the soundtrack of our relationship people would have to feel the vibrations of it, I make this suggestion, "You should record it. Share our story."

"I'm not sure other people would understand." Albert pulls the bag from the waste bin and ties it tight. Rhythmically, he shakes another bag and drops it in, pulling it over the edges of the bin. "I suppose it wouldn't matter."

"You can have Lia help you with it."

Frequency 16

"Would you like that?"

"I would. Especially since you remember what she looks like so vividly."

I genuinely mean it. The look that settles on his perfect face fills me with something I think might be joy. I felt it a few times before. This Lia makes him feel complete; something even I could never do. All I ever wanted was for him to be whole. To actually live.

"I think I'm in love with her." Albert smiles. "I always think about the inflections and vibrations of her voice."

"Does she know about me? I mean *all* about me?"

"Actually, she does," he confesses. I know he has never told anyone else about me. About us. It's all been too sacred – until now. He looks at me as he tilts his head and sighs. He always does that when he's reluctantly conceding something to me. "I'm going to have to choose between you."

"Yes, it's probably time."

"Yeah."

We study each other, and I consider the inner struggle he's reconciling now. He's letting go of the last threads of this desperate notion that he can find a way to get back those sixteen minutes. This belief he's held on to for as long as I can remember, that he can't function without me. The truth is, I could never function without him. My wonderful, charming, talented Albert releases beautiful, positive things into the world just by living. I have one great legacy. Still, I wait... and smile as I see the peace finally settle over him.

"Take me home, Al."

"Are you sure?"

"Yes, we're both ready." I wait while he puts on a jacket and tennis shoes. When he's dressed, I tuck the picture into his breast pocket. "Take this with you. It'll be okay."

He only nods.

It's goodbye. His hands tremble as he finds his keys in the bowl on the desk. He sorts through them looking for the car key as he leaves the kitchen and opens the garage door. He doesn't even look back to make sure I'm coming. I'm proud of him. So proud.

We say nothing as he starts the car, waits for the garage door to lift, and backs out of the driveway. As he drives through the city, I watch the shifting colors of the sky, the silhouettes of the passing homes in the twilight. I know we're making this drive for the last time.

We reach the gate as the clock reads five forty-three am. Albert opens the window and pushes the call button.

"Yeah." A man's voice, half-asleep, crackles over the speaker. "Who's there?"

"It's uh. It's me, Steve."

"*Albert?* What time is it?" The voice on the other side of the box slowly orients itself.

"Five forty-four. And sixteen seconds."

After a pause, the gate buzzes open, and Al slowly drives through the sleepy neighborhood. He's not even aware of me as he pulls the car up to the house. I disappear behind a hydrangea as he walks to the door and waits.

When Steve opens the door, he's still rubbing the sleep from his eyes. He's wearing my favorite pyjama pants, green flannel with corgies wearing sunglasses. Even with bed hair and yesterday's stubble, he takes my breath away.

"Are you okay, Al?" he asks with genuine concern.

"Um. Yes, I'm good. I've just been up all night." He shifts on his feet and studies the peony bushes beside the porch. "Those have a good, calm frequency."

"You think so?" Steve steps out of the doorway onto the porch and leans on the railing.

"I do."

"She planted those the day she found out," he says.

"Oh! Uh, yeah." Albert looks at them a little longer while Steve patiently waits for him to say something else. I think they study the peonies for a food five minutes before Albert says, "I broke the glass tonight."

"Did you?" he asks quietly. "Are you okay with that?"

"Yeah," Albert shrugs. He leans against the opposite railing, arms crossed over his chest, staring at the planks under his feet. "I'm going to write her music."

"That's a good thing. Can I hear it when you're finished?"

"Yeah. Yeah, I think she would have liked that."

"Thank you." He smiles at Albert and opens the door a crack to listen for something.

Albert shifts on his feet again. "So, I met someone."

"Did you?"

"Yeah." He studies the peonies again as he tries to make this conversation. "She. Well. She's got a calming frequency."

"Maybe you can bring her around some time. You know you're always welcome." Steve closes the door and leans on the rail again.

"I know."

"Just think about it," he suggests. "I know that's a big step for you."

There's a long, unusually comfortable silence. Albert reaches into his jacket pocket and pulls out the picture. He looks at it again before he hands it to Steve. "Is this me or…?"

"That's Mandy; Aunt Jane took it a few weeks ago. You look so much alike, you could be twins." He points to the picture and explains, "That's her drum. She made it out of Amanda's old photo box."

"That's our Nana's hatbox," Albert corrects.

"Ah. Well, she's always making sound patterns, so when I found that in the attic I thought it might be okay."

"It has good resonances. I started on it about the same age." Taking the picture back, he tucks it into his pocket. He rakes his hair with his fingers and takes a few deep breaths. "I miss Amanda."

"Me too." He stands with one arm in the door and the rest of himself on the porch. "I know it's not the same with me as it is for you. Maybe it sounds stupid, but after three years I still find myself talking to her."

"Yeah."

"Sometimes it's like she's right beside me." Steve's voice is cracking, and I want to tell him I'm here but I can't. "I wish I could bring her back."

"Three years." Albert stares at the peonies to avoid looking at Steve. His brows knit. He's thinking, trying to relate to my husband's pain. These are emotions I know he doesn't understand, but he makes the sweetest effort. "Before..., there were only sixteen minutes we had ever been apart."

"I envy you. What I wouldn't give to be able to say that."

"I can't get those sixteen minutes back. Ever."

"No, you can't. But you had twenty-seven years after that sixteen minutes to make up for it."

"Twenty-six years, ten months, five days, nineteen hours. And 48 minutes." Albert thinks for a moment. His brow knits in that way he has when he's been wounded. "Our mom always said those were Amanda's sixteen minutes of freedom."

Thanks a lot, Lena.

I have no relationship with that woman, and I don't regret it. What kind of mother has the nerve to think something like that, let alone say it to her son?

She was always spewing crap like that when she could have been appreciating him or getting him some help. Instead, she passed us off as her embarrassingly defiant daughter and her "special" son. She had no idea that my defiant posture began as a way to protect him from her. Dad eventually left her and filed for full custody of us. She never fought it. Every six months, she'd show up and pretend to be the mother of the year, but all that did was stress everyone out. Before my wedding, we hadn't seen her since she destroyed Albert's laundry. None of us have heard from her since.

Steve has never liked the way she treats Al either. I've told him how deeply the stupid crap she's said has affected him, but he doesn't let on. Instead, he tells Albert my deepest, most cherished secret.

"Amanda never felt that way. She told me she probably spent those minutes making sure the frequency was right for you."

Yes, I really do believe that.

"I never thought of it like that." It's clear by his tone of voice that he hasn't. He only enjoys the healing that truth gives him until dread washes over him. He palms his forehead as his shoulders droop. "It must have been an awful burden on her all those years, taking care of me."

"Not at all. She missed you when you stopped coming around. We both did." He

Frequency 16

watches Albert's jaw set as he processes everything. I knew this day would come, and I knew Steve would be gentle with him. He waits patiently while Albert processes all the new information until his attention is drawn to the house. "Al, would you like to come in and let me know if the house has a good frequency for Mandy?" Waiting to see what Albert will do, Steve opens the door the rest of the way. "Maybe you can help me set it right."

"I'd like…that."   He steps into the house and immediately freezes.

"Sorry, Pumpkin," Steve's gentle voice fills the entryway from behind him. Stepping around Albert, Steve approaches our little girl standing at the foot of the staircase. She really does look just like Al. "I hope we didn't wake you up."

Mandy shakes her head, never taking her eyes off of Albert. He begins to fidget as they standoff in the hallway. She's such a serious little general in her pink footy pajamas. He reluctantly obeys Steve's urging to follow him before he stops again. Standing almost completely still, Albert studies Mandy for a moment before he waves nervously.

"Hello."

Somewhere in the house, a faucet drips. The sound softly echoes.

"Hello," she mimics, raising her hand the same way. She's like him in so many ways, it's uncanny.

"You're Mandy?"

"Yeah," she answers suspiciously, as she studies Albert in turn. "I'm three."

"I'm thirty."

"You look like my mama," she says tilting her head in the same way he does.

"Yes, she um..."

"She died."

"Yeah. She did," he manages. I'm sure this is the first time he's acknowledged the fact, and he has no idea what else to say. He looks to Steve who nods for him to go on. "She's my. I'm. I'm your uncle."

"Albert?" Her big green eyes light up and she smiles. "Really!?"

"Yeah." He shuffles his feet and stuffs his hands in his pockets. "So, uh. Can I see your drum?"

Frequency 16

It takes sixteen seconds for Mandy to take Albert by his hand and pull him into the dining room. His smile is sublime as she points to where Nana's hatbox sits under the table, an assortment of spoons, rulers, chopsticks, and brushes on the floor beside it. As they crawl under, hidden by the linen cloth, Steve quietly disappears into the kitchen.

Slowly, steadily, they begin to experiment with rhythms and sounds. As they create their new vibration, I feel my brother let me go for the first time. Ever. It's such a strange thing; if I didn't know my place was in the Cloud, I'd be afraid. By the time Steve comes back with coffee, I'm sure I'll be gone.

ABOUT THE AUTHOR

h.e. newell

Thanks so much for reading this story. I am so in love with it. On the other side of every loss, struggle, or hard time I have ever had, there has been a deep, beautiful healing. Relationships restored, namely between myself and the Lord. Jesus is so good.

. My prayer for you is that you will find your perfect frequency no matter what you are experiencing. Please feel free to send me a note. Let me know how I can be praying for you. Let me know what Jesus is doing with you.

throneroomjewel@gmail.com

Made in the USA
Columbia, SC
01 March 2022